VIRGINIA

By the same author

Silence in October
Lucca

VIRGINIA

Jens Christian Grøndahl

Translated by Anne Born

CANONGATE

First published in Great Britain in 2003
by Canongate Books Ltd,
14 High Street, Edinburgh EH1 1TE.
First published in Danish in 2000 by
Rosinante, Copenhagen.

10 9 8 7 6 5 4 3 2 1

British Library Cataloguing-in-Publication Data
A catalogue record for this book is available on
request from the British Library.

ISBN 1 84195 410 1

Typeset by Palimpsest Book Production Ltd,
Polmont, Stirlingshire
Printed and bound by
Nørhaven Paperback A/S, Denmark

www.canongate.net

You could never get used to the sound, the distant drone of aircraft engines passing high overhead in the night. It was hot under the sloping timber roof, and she kept her window open. She lay with one leg outside the duvet, breathing in the stuffy holiday cottage air and feeling the cool breeze on her calf and thigh, listening to the small dry click when the wooden edge of the black-out curtain bumped against the window-frame. She'd just had her sixteenth birthday that summer, the only time she stayed at the house by the sea. She didn't belong here. She slipped out of our life and we slipped out of hers.

Every night she waited for the planes. She wasn't afraid, she knew they wouldn't drop any bombs here, where there was nothing but beach and fjord and scattered houses. To start with, the sound could hardly be distinguished from the beat of the waves behind the sand dunes. Shortly afterwards it flew over the roof the sun had heated up in the course of the day, so the room was heavy with stale air, the smell of dust, mattress and forgotten summers. Many years later she said that smell always reminded her of the war. She is dead now. I am the only one able to piece the story together after a fashion. Only she and I knew about it, and for years we only knew our own side of it.

The house is still there. Several more cottages have been built around it, but at that time it stood by itself, a little apart from the cluster of houses beside the road, where there was a grocer's shop and a pub. The countryside has not changed, the sea and the beach, the dunes with marram grass and the semi-flooded stretch of meadow-land running inwards behind the coastline, at the end of the fjord. There are the same tufts and grass-covered tongues of land crowded with birds, taking off above the quiet water and gathering between the clouds and the water surface in flashing flocks that remind you of huge, revolving radar screens.

She was not familiar with this part of the country. Brought up in Copenhagen, she had lived there alone with her mother in a small flat near the harbour for as long as she could remember. Her father had left them when she was a month or two old, she had never met him. Her mother worked at home, she was a dressmaker. Half the living room was taken up by the big table with the sewing machine, clothes stands, dressmaker's dummies and shelves for bolts of cloth. When one of her mother's customers came she had to do her homework in the kitchen. Sometimes she withdrew to the small bedroom, where their beds stood, so close to each other and the walls so that you had to edge between them sideways. In the evenings they cleared half the table so there was a space for them to eat, the mother and the daughter – the daughter who stayed at a house beside the North Sea one summer listening to the sound of the waves behind the dunes and the English aeroplanes.

Maybe she would think about her mother, who had stayed in town. Maybe she would think about the flat they lived in, and the things she had known as far back as she could remember. The shining wheel of the sewing machine and the heavy scissors on the work table. The view between the house plants to the block opposite and the view from the bedroom, which looked onto the courtyard. The sweetish rotten smell of rubbish from down there in summer. The fog that descended in autumn like a grey veil in front of the grey walls and dark windows. The sound of ships' fog horns out in the Sound, muffled and long drawn out, like an empty bottle makes when you blow into it.

One afternoon her mother had knocked at

the bedroom door as she sat on her bed reading. Her mother didn't usually knock. She asked her to come in for a moment, her voice sounded almost polite. A lady sat in the living room, she had passed the time of day with her several times before. One of her mother's regular customers. The lady had been kind enough, her mother said, to ask whether she might like to spend the summer holidays with her and her husband.

She didn't understand, she had only spoken a few times to the strange woman and then only to answer the usual questions about school. Nor could she understand her mother, who suddenly seemed like a stranger herself. She wondered at the way her mother introduced the surprising offer with: 'had been kind enough . . .'. They could hardly look each other in the eye, she and her mother, who sat on the edge of her chair with her hands in her lap and drooping shoulders. The other woman had already put on her hat.

'We have to help each other, don't we?' she said. She had painted lips, they smiled between her vigorous cheeks, as if by their own volition. As if the smile was a kind of involuntary twitch in her otherwise motionless face.

Sitting in the train, the girl thought of her mother, and later, when she lay awake at night in the cramped bedroom they assigned to her. They had emptied a drawer in the chest where she could put her clothes. The drawer rattled so loudly it must have been audible all over the house. She thought of the little flat near the harbour as the train carried her through the landscape.

At that time the journey took the best part of a day. You could hardly see there was a war on. Only at the stations and in the brief glimpses of streets beside the railway lines passing through the provincial towns could you catch a glimpse of the strange uniforms and military vehicles now and then. It was the same landscape as before and then later, with corn fields and forest and water sparkling in the sunshine.

As she looked out at it she thought of her mother's frail shoulders, the grey hairs in her chignon and the sewing-machine wheel in the semi-twilight of the room at early evening, when the sun was only an afterglow on the façades opposite. After the lady left they had eaten, without speaking much, as usual.

'Well, that is one way,' her mother had said as they washed up. The summer could seem so long in town.

A powerfully built man in a light suit and straw hat met her at the station. He picked up her suitcase and carried it out to a large open-topped car. She noticed he was wearing driving gloves of pale-coloured leather.

He had built the holiday cottage after the earlier war, when he had been appointed a consultant surgeon. He and his wife had never had children, but for a number of years they asked their nephew to stay every summer in the red-painted wooden house by the North Sea. They might have invited the dress-maker's daughter on holiday to keep him company, the lanky fourteen-year-old boy who lay on his stomach in a sand dune watching the car stop in front of the house and the strange girl getting out. The consultant held the door for her, his straw hat in his hand, like a hotel porter, with the afternoon sun shining on his bald pate.

She was broad-shouldered and had long arms and strong legs. She looked like a swimmer. Her summer dress was blue, she had bare shoulders and loose flaxen hair, which flew out behind her when she walked in the wind and the sunshine which made the marram grass glisten and sparkle. Her cheekbones were broad and her eyes blue, but he didn't notice that until later, when he came down from his dune.

Her arrival had been announced a week earlier. He might already have had a presentiment of what it would feel like, the first time her blue eyes rested on him, briefly and expressionlessly. They had sat down to dinner and she replied to the questions they asked her about her journey and about herself, just as expressionlessly, but politely. He didn't allow himself to look at the new arrival for more than a few seconds at a time. If he had known how she saw him it would have confirmed his worst forebodings.

She thought he looked funny with his bony body, close-set eyes and the wiry hair that constantly fell over his forehead even though he tried to comb it back with water. He hadn't had much to do with girls yet, hardly anything in fact. He couldn't look at them without feeling doomed. But they must have overcome their embarrassed silence, the young woman and the overgrown boy. A couple of years' difference can be enough to decide which words to use. Woman. Boy.

When they were older they couldn't remember what they had talked about that summer. They probably told each other what they had managed to experience, considering how young they were. Perhaps they also discussed what they imagined might happen to them when they grew up and the war was over.

The conversations beside the sea had faded out and the words been forgotten. Only the sea and the beach remained, and the recollection by one of them that they had once walked together on the far side of all the years that would pass before they met again. But they could both remember lying on the beach and swimming together when the breakers were not too fierce. His aunt warned them again and again of the undertow. He was a good swimmer, in the water they were equals, but when they came out onto the beach he was again aware she was older than he was.

Many years later he told her he had suspected she had been friendly towards him only because in her eyes he was harmless, and then because he was her hosts' nephew. She smiled when he said that but made no reply, and he came to think of the way she smiled and her expression that grew more preoccupied during the short time they spent together. She seemed so pensive when they walked beside the waves or sat on the beach playing with the sand that trickled between their fingers, until someone called her from the house.

There was no question of duties, come to that. It had been her own idea to lend a hand in the kitchen. The housekeeper was an elderly woman with thin lips and big hands. The consultant's wife had actually taken the girl aside and said she must remember she was a guest. She had replied that she didn't mind helping. She joined in preparing dinner and serving it before she sat down in her place at table and the housekeeper withdrew to the kitchen. Then she hastened to spread her napkin on her lap like the others. She was given her own silver napkin ring like theirs. They used the same napkins for several days before they were changed and washed and hung out to dry on the clothes-line behind the house among sheets and shirts.

She loved to sniff in the scent of clean linen that had hung on the line in the wind. Once he saw her, lost in meditation as she could be, engaged in taking in the laundry. She stood there behind the house with her face buried in a sheet. She saw him looking at her and he saw her cheeks blush slightly. He lowered his own eyes, but it had been strangely exciting to feel the unexpected power of his glance.

Perhaps he even confused it with the feeling of having stolen something from her, something he could take away with him and keep, one evening when she hadn't bothered to close the bathroom window. She couldn't see him out there in the twilight, herself white and indistinct in the dark bathroom, lifting her large, soft breasts gently and intimately to dry underneath them with her towel. Later, when the wet towel hung flapping by itself on the empty clothes-line, he couldn't resist holding it up to his face. But then he only felt powerless again, and dropped it at once, afraid of being seen from inside the house.

She didn't see him. When he was not present

she did not think of him. She only saw him if he was actually there, but not because she wanted him to be there. She just didn't give him a thought. Later on she could not remember what she had thought about during the weeks before her sudden departure, in the strange house in company with strange people she had not herself chosen to spend summer with. She could remember lying awake at night, and often thinking about her mother without actually missing her. She thought about the woman who happened to be her mother, and about the cramped, dark flat near the harbour that was her home.

She heard the bombers flying over Denmark and imagined them flying above the city and dropping their cargo. Perhaps one of the bombs would hit the block they lived in, and crash down through the living-room ceiling. Her mother would be sitting in the shelter down in the cellar as the bomb hit their home and the rest of the block and brought it crashing down in a cloud of rubble. They had been in the shelter several times with the other residents on the staircase when there was an air-raid warning. Some of them had been in night clothes and dressing gowns. Nothing had ever happened. The war went on somewhere else, far out behind the black-out curtains. It consisted of sounds, voices on the wireless and rumours in the street, sirens from the rooftops and the distant drone of the aircraft engines approaching from out at sea.

They must have cycled out more than once to the half-submerged meadows at the end of the fjord. He had often been there alone, both that summer and in earlier ones. The horizon ran almost full circle, broken only by a spruce plantation to the south, scattered clumps of reeds and the sand dunes to the west. Furthest out on an isthmus there was a wooden shed made of grooved planks. You had to leave the bicycles and continue on foot for the last stretch along the water-logged strips of earth.

He showed her how you could get right out to the shed by taking a detour. It stood out like a solitary figure surrounded by cloud masses and their gliding reflections in the calm water, a distance so far it was hard to understand how anyone could have transported the long planks so far out or thought of building a shed out there at all.

When you turned round you could see nothing but water, grass and sky, where the meadows blended into the fjord. They stood quite still listening to the wind and the birds. There were narrow chinks between the planks of the shed, which dispersed the light into transparent fans. If you put your eye to the chinks you could look out. She was standing like that, with her eye to the crack between two planks, when he walked over to her and placed a timid hand on her back, just above the small of it. Later he could not comprehend how he'd had the courage. She had turned and thrown him a brief glance of surprised amusement before she pressed a forefinger to his nose and went outside.

She overtook him as they cycled back along the narrow path with flooded grass on both sides. Her frock tightened around her hips when she trod down on the pedals and her smooth calves shone in the sun. She had a large birthmark at the back of one knee, you could see it every time she stretched her leg. It seemed like a blemish, but at the same time it drew all his attention to the fleeting glimpses he had of the backs of her knees when they came in sight by turns beneath her fluttering skirts. He felt he had to get in front again, after all he was the one who knew the place, and he rode up beside her. She cried out, there wasn't room for two bicycles on the path and next moment he lost his balance. There was nothing in the least spiteful or malicious about her laughter. She merely laughed as he stood up, soaking wet and covered with mud. She laughed in the way he imagined a sister might have done.

He was aware of her every movement around the house. He listened for her steps on the stairs and the door of her room when it was closed, cautiously, he felt. It would be wrong to say she avoided him, but neither did she seek him out. Certainly it occurred to him that she might only have gone for walks on the beach or bicycle rides with him because she was a guest in the house. A guest who compensated for the hospitality she enjoyed by peeling potatoes and hanging up the washing and on the whole making as little noise as possible, and who thus saw it as one of her duties to keep him company. But that might just as well have been something he merely imagined.

She was consistently friendly, even after the afternoon in the shed out there in the water meadows, maybe a touch more detached, maybe not even that. She was so reserved and polite, both to him and to his uncle and aunt.

He thought she hid herself behind her smile and her modesty, her readiness to help with domestic tasks and her efforts to sit nicely at table. At the beginning he had noticed her several times propping her knife and fork against the edge of her plate. She had pulled herself up and put them correctly on the plate itself when she saw his aunt's slightly forced smile. He knew almost nothing about her. She had not told him anything except quite ordinary things about herself and that made her all the more baffling.

One late afternoon when she was down in the kitchen he went into her room. He looked at the things lying around, a young woman's belongings and clothes, nothing special. He caught sight of himself in the spotted mirror above the wash basin, where the evening sun shone dimly and metallically around a dark, obscure figure without a face.

It might have been that night they heard the English planes again. The depressing, uniform drone was suddenly interrupted by a snarl that increased in strength and was abruptly silenced, to be followed shortly afterwards by a muffled crash like distant thunder.

Early next morning he went out again to sit in the nearest sand dune and observe her through the open bathroom window. He had just woken up when he heard her bare feet on the varnished stairs. He sneaked round the other side of the house after eventually plucking up courage, if it was courage that drove him, and not something else even stronger than his timidity. The sun had just risen above the roof and he had to shade his eyes with a hand. Suddenly she bent forward, her breasts hanging heavily for a moment beneath her forward-leaning torso. The window was closed with a bang.

He went down onto the beach. When he came back her bicycle had disappeared. He tried to picture what it would be like when she came back and he had to look her in the eye. If he left her to herself and was merely passive when she returned, it would seem like an admission that he had spied on her. He would have to find her and somehow convince her that it had been nothing like that, in fact. That it was a case of misunderstanding, a chance, unfortunate coincidence that he had been sitting in the marram grass when she happened to be in the bathroom. He had to do something, because even if he made things worse that would be better than doing nothing.

The thought struck him that she might have gone out to the meadows. He was through the plantation and on the other side of it when he saw her walking towards him, far away out there. He hid himself in the murk of the close-set pines until she had cycled past. A sunlit, unapproachable, energetic figure on the sunken road leading to the village. She was up in her room when he got home.

Later on, when they were at the breakfast table, she seemed her usual self, smiling in her nicely behaved manner. And perhaps nothing out of the way had happened, after all . . . His uncle reported hearing that an English aircraft had crashed somewhere to the north, near the sea. There was a photograph, taken on the same or one of the following days by a local photographer. A German soldier stood guard over the wrecked plane, you could glimpse the twisted iron struts that had braced the glass cage of the cockpit, and a piece of the wing with a double, dotted and dashed line, bent and broken, where the plates had been riveted together. On the wing were two concentric painted circles: the emblem of the *Royal Air Force.*

The consultant asked them if they had heard it. He himself had been woken up by the sound. The girl did not react but listened attentively to him, recounting the villagers' description of it. She kept to herself that day, but maybe it was only because he dared not go near her. Maybe everything would have been normal if he had dared. At dinner the consultant told them that a parachute had been found drifting out in the fjord.

She went up to her room earlier than usual. When he too had gone to bed he lay listening as usual to the creaking of her bedsprings as they sank under her weight. He expected her to brush the timber wall with a toe, an elbow or a knee, as if to touch him. His aunt was still downstairs listening to the radio. In the silence he could hear the muffled music. He pictured the girl's body beside him in the darkness on the other side of the wall, so close that he could reach out and touch her.

She lies awake listening in the silence. She listens to the woodwork relaxing after being warmed by the sun, the squeaking tap and running water in the room on the other side of the corridor, where the consultant is cleaning his teeth. Then he too goes to bed.

The housekeeper has already retired for the night but the lady of the house is still down in the sitting room with the wireless set, under the lamp that sheds its light in vain on the matt black-out curtain, as if the window looks out onto a mountain wall.

The muffled dance music penetrates through ceiling and wall timbers to the young woman lying in the dark listening. Cool lingering music, like the breeze from the open window, she thinks, and visualises the mature woman, in the dark crimson armchair, her hands on its arms, gazing at the woven panel of the loudspeaker. She wears a white blouse and a long, pleated skirt and silk stockings, as if dressed for town. As if she had just come home after an evening at a restaurant where you can dance to an orchestra playing that kind of music.

The two women listen to the softly flowing strings and saxophones playing for whoever is awake at this hour around the blacked-out land. They listen to the same music, but the older woman thinks she is listening alone. That she is the only one picturing a dance floor in town, brilliantly lit, with gliding figures, the men in dark clothes, the women with sparkling necklaces, in long dresses that swing around them like flower-heads, fans or wings.

The girl waits for the music to die down. Then she listens for the other woman's steps, the sound of running water in the bathroom pipes and the long silence before her hostess finally comes upstairs and gently opens and closes the door of her room. The consultant and his wife have separate rooms. The girl waits for a while longer, after the silence is no longer disturbed by anything except the slight rattling of the black-out curtain in the breeze from the open window. Probably half an hour passes, perhaps the best part of an hour, before she dares leave her bed, cautiously, as she braces her arms against the springs to quieten them and not give herself away. She gets dressed in the dark and slowly presses down the latch so she can open the door soundlessly. She knows which of the stair treads creak.

While she helped prepare the evening meal she secretly filled a basket and hid it in the woodshed. The key of the kitchen door clicks slightly. She stands and waits before slowly pushing the door open. It sticks a bit and she barely closes it after her, without pushing down the handle. She has left her bicycle a little way away from the house. No one will be able to hear her when she mounts it and cycles out onto the road.

It is a clear, light night and she has no trouble finding her way through the blue landscape. Only when she rides through the plantation does it get so dark she can barely see the track. She has to look up and follow the opening between the topmost branches of the pines where the sky makes a blue path in the blackness with a slim moon and a few stars.

Like a watercourse, she thinks, running into the sea, when she comes out into the open again and goes on along the path surrounded by flooded grass. Soon she can clearly distinguish the shed out there beneath the sharp edge of the moon, floating likewise in all the blue.

When she had cycled there in the morning the low sun shone sharply on the faded white planks. A golden point was clearly reflected in the water among the tiny outlines of the grass blades in the smooth motionless surface. Swallows circled around the place like a swarm of arrow-heads, rising into the air and descending with a sudden jerk. She could not have known she would go back there the same night, fearful that someone might catch sight of her, and equally fearful of her own resolve. She had not even hit on the deserted shed as her goal when she mounted her bicycle in the morning. She just wanted to be alone riding out into the blue, which was why she had ended up seeking the most solitary place she could think of. You nearly always met someone on the beach, but not here.

She left the bicycle where the path began to get smaller, and continued on foot along the narrow track to the shed. She sat down with her back to the wall and closed her eyes. The grass was damp but the sun had already warmed the planks, and she felt the heat on her back. The swallows flew around her in closer and more distant circles. Their cries sounded like the singing invisible hinges of a thousand unseen doors opening and closing.

Later she couldn't remember how long she had sat like that when she heard something else. It might have been a sigh as she herself drew breath, or a heel scraping on the dry earth in there. Perhaps an involuntary shrug of the shoulders caused a plank to creak, or a faint snore. She imagined they must have been sitting shoulder to shoulder, as if leaning against a mirror.

She stood still for a moment in the doorway

to allow her eyes to accustom themselves to the transition from the bright morning sunshine to the semi-darkness inside. She thought it might be an animal she had heard, a hedgehog or a fox. Slowly she began to make out the interior of the shed, where the sunlight seeped through the vertical cracks in the wall in wings and fans of light. He sat huddled in a corner, asleep.

The night air is cool on her arms and legs. The damp soil drags at her shoes, which make a sucking sound at each step as she walks towards the dark doorway of the shed, basket in hand. She knows she is being watched. A dim figure in a crack between the planks. She cannot see him now but she knows where he is and she knows he is watching her against the section of sky in the doorway.

He calls to her softly. He speaks to her in his soft voice in the foreign language she partly understands but herself can only voice in the simplest way. She is no longer afraid when he cautiously reaches out for her arm and slides his hand along its underside until it finds the basket. She squats down opposite the dark figure in the corner and listens to him ravenously devouring the food.

She tries to see the face in front of her in the morning sunlight that brushes his stubble and the hair flopping down over his forehead. The dried mud on his cheeks and his hunched body in the filthy, damp pilot's suit. The shining green of his eyes when he'd suddenly opened them and looked into hers. She remembers her surprise when his lips, from one second to another, almost parted in a smile, as if he had seen an angel.

She didn't say much more about it. No one knows what they said to one another.

She lay awake again the following night waiting in the silence before creeping out of the house with her basket. She did not know someone had heard her. He saw her from the window as she cycled out along the road. He dressed hurriedly and ran up onto one of the nearest sand dunes, from where he could see her, far off but quite clearly in the light night. She turned off the road just before the village and vanished into the plantation. He followed her on his bicycle and hid himself among the dense pine trees. He waited until he saw her reappear in the deserted landscape, wheeling her bicycle and mounting it only when she approached and passed his motionless figure in the darkness beneath the thick foliage of the low-growing branches.

She avoided him again the following day. After breakfast she went out into the dunes with a book. She went on reading when he found her and sat down beside her. He tried to start a conversation but she merely gave him a brief glance before lowering her eyes to her book again. He apologised to her. She looked at him again, and the slight twitch at the corner of her mouth seemed like a smile. What for? He thought of her breasts, their soft white weight when she had bent over the previous morning to close the window with a bang. The thought and her gaze, the cool merriment behind her faint surprise, made him blush.

He got up to leave, injured and ridiculous at once, but could not help looking back at her. She sat with her back towards him, surrounded by the restless marram grass in the wind. She sat with her book on her lap looking out over the waves to the horizon, as the wind snatched at the marram and at her hair. He picked up his bicycle and cycled off along the road and turned in through the plantation.

I can no longer differentiate between what he did not know and what, after many years had passed, I heard about it. I cannot describe what he had in mind when he left his bicycle lying on the damp grass and continued on foot along the narrow path to the shed standing there as if on a desert island surrounded by water and sky. He hesitated in the doorway as if sensing he was being watched. No sound came from within and at first he could not see anything when he stepped inside into the semi-darkness.

You do not remember your thoughts, you think of something else instead when you tentatively try to recall what you have forgotten. But I recall the shock when he heard voices from outside and at the same moment was seized in a hard grip by a hand that came out of the semi-darkness and pulled him down. The stranger smelled of earth and sweat, and in the strip of light infiltrating between two planks a face came in sight with wide eyes and a threatening expression. The voices outside grew plainer as they approached. One of them laughed. In the crack between the planks he caught sight of two German soldiers walking along the path towards the shed.

The pilot loosened his grip. They looked at each other as they listened to the approaching voices. The man's green eyes fixed him with a hard stare, without blinking. The boy lowered his gaze but could still feel the other looking at him. An empty milk bottle and half a slice of bread lay on the ground. The strip of light pierced the whitish film on the inside of the bottle.

She had brought him milk and bread when she found him after he had fallen from the sky and hidden himself here, and she had come back. She thought about him when she sat in a sand dune with a book on her lap and looked out over the sea, aloof and unapproachable. She had planned to go back to the stranger in the shed when darkness fell again.

The German soldiers had stopped on the other side of the planked wall. He could hear their voices quite clearly now but couldn't understand what they said. When he looked up again the pilot gestured excitedly at him as if to urge him away, out of the shed to where the soldiers were coming round the corner to the doorway.

He did not move while the other repeated his desperate, soundless gesture. Not a single thought passed through his mind in the seconds that followed, but through all the succeeding years I have asked myself whether the German soldiers had seen me go into the shed and whether it would have made any difference if I had gone out to them alone instead of letting them find us together.

Maybe they would have searched the place anyway. On the other hand it is not impossible that they might merely have laughed at the terrified boy who came out of his hiding place before they went on along the path, while in fact the boy stayed there watching them and holding his breath. The possibility has stayed with me always, like a thought I have never been able to think through to the end and so have never finished.

She had already left when my uncle and aunt had fetched me after the interrogation and we were back at the house. She had left a letter, my aunt read it and passed it to my uncle. I went down to the beach. Maybe she had imagined that in some way or other she could save him. As time passed it all came to seem like a dream, but all the same I had to defend myself at night when I lay sleepless. I listed everything that could serve as an excuse. My young age and the pilot's already hazardous and hopeless situation. The impossibility of two young people being able to smuggle him across country and on board one of the fishing smacks which illegally transported resistance people and Jews across to Sweden.

I kept on telling myself that he must surely have been treated as a prisoner of war and sent to a camp in Germany, where most of the prisoners did survive. That he probably went back to England after the war, emaciated but alive, then married and had children like everyone else. But nothing helped. In her eyes I had betrayed them both, her blue eyes that looked at me with a searching, expectant expression as I lay awake. And deep down I knew she was right, because I could just have kept away from that shed.

Several times after the summer holidays I found my way to her street near the harbour. Just once when I was standing in a gateway I saw her come out from her stairway and walk along the pavement, beautiful and alone. I followed her at a distance through the streets beside the railway that separated her district from the harbour area. I can clearly see her upright figure in a summer dress that flowed around her hips and kept pace with her stride. I see her sun-tanned arms and her hair shining brightly each time she walks out of the shadow.

She strolls with slow steps past the tobacconist's and the bicycle mechanic's in the small square round the corner. She goes on along the streets, seemingly aimless until finally she walks through the open glass door of the elevated railway. There is a view from the platform over the wharves, ships and warehouses beside the docks. I have to be content to imagine her standing on the platform looking out over the Sound.

Most likely she was thinking about the English pilot. Many years later she said that had been the first time a man touched her. He had caressed her face and hair and hesitated a little before she slowly bent her face towards him and felt his stubble and lips. A single slow, tentative kiss. That was the whole of their love story.

He had searched his breast pocket for something and slid a flat metal object into her hand, it was cool. Afterwards she thought he must have felt sure they wouldn't meet again. It was a silver cigarette case, and there was just one cigarette left. A yellowing elastic strap keeps it in place, never smoked in all this time. The surface of the case is dull and grey, it has not been polished for so many years. His initials are delineated in the slightly curved, engraved lid: *M.W.* A few ochre and reddish-brown shreds of tobacco have crumbled and sifted out of the cylinder-shaped paper container and come to rest in one of the curved corners of the case.

She sent it to me a year ago when she realised the way things were going. That was how she put it. It was the only letter I had from her after our reunion, and she specifically wrote that I was not to reply. She was already ill when we met, but I had not known that then. On the whole we knew hardly anything about each other, only what I am recording here. We belonged to an early episode in each other's youth, disconnected from the life we would come to live, and which perhaps for the same reason we only discussed with sporadic comments.

I recognised her tone of voice in the letter, brief and unsentimental, with no suggestion of originality or personal characteristic even when it was dealing with the most serious things as, for instance, her own approaching death. As if she wanted to say in this indirect way that death least of all is anything special. When I received the package with the cigarette case and her letter it was almost four years since we had met, apart from once when we came across each other in Strøget at the end of the Fifties.

She must have been just over thirty, but I recognised her at once, even though she had turned into a lady in a smart suit. She knew me too and seemed glad to see me. We stood in the middle of the stream of cars and people, she was in a hurry. She had married and had a child. They were going to move to Paris, she told me and said I should contact her if I ever came that way.

I had not expected to see her again, and many years went by before I took her at her word. I had just retired, and a few years earlier I had been divorced from my second wife. It was a rare occurrence for me to get together with the son and daughter of my first marriage, although I really believe they have gradually forgiven me for whatever they had to forgive. We leave each other in peace, and I only mention my family to explain that for the first time I was alone and absolutely free to do as I pleased.

It was the beginning of May and I decided to realise an old dream of spending a month in Paris. I had not been there since I was on honeymoon with my first wife a good forty years ago. I have never managed to travel as much as I might have wanted, and meanwhile my wanderlust has waned. Shortly after my son was born we bought a holiday cottage, where I stayed almost every weekend and holiday even after I was divorced the first time, when the children had left home.

We had stayed at a small hotel in the Rue du Dragon. It was still there, but our old room on the top floor was occupied, so I had one overlooking the courtyard. In the nature of things the view wasn't anything to write home about except that I could see right into the room opposite when the light was switched on behind the flimsy curtains. It was quieter than facing the street and I could stay there as long as it suited me. The room opposite changed occupants several times during my stay. Fleeting figures, usually with their backs turned, came in sight behind the transparent white curtains when the shutters were not closed.

Actually I did not feel the city had changed

very much. The streets looked the same with their pale grey façades and shutters and plane trees and open-air cafés with wide awnings and glass fronts. Perhaps I am remembering wrongly, Paris has surely changed as much as I have. There were many people from other parts of the world and, as in all other towns, there was always someone standing alone on the pavement talking into a mobile phone.

I made a habit of seeking out a new district every day and set off systematically. I stuck a map on the wall with tape and marked with a ball-pen where I had been and along which streets I had walked. In this way my picture of Paris grew day by day into a pattern whose lines at first hardly touched each other, until they wove themselves together into ever more complicated knots and loops.

The feeling of being pushed into a pocket in the big city did me good. I could lie for ages in bed looking up at the sky through the narrow shaft between the courtyard walls towards an approaching rain cloud. I thought how it might already be raining over the northern districts, and that from above everything must look like a stone colossus intersected by cracks that divided and met in clustered constellations.

I like walking and can still keep going for a long time without getting tired. I didn't visit museums, that has never appealed to me. I have gone to museums only when forced to, at school or if one of the women I have been married to insisted on seeing some exhibition. Moreover I do not care to be in a crowd of other tourists, but probably no tourist does. I may be wrong. In any case I prefer districts where people just live and ply their trade or go on everyday errands. I like sitting over a beer watching them pass by and being outside it all and yet a part of the changing street scene, anonymous and easy to overlook.

I am pretty certain that I made the decision to go to Paris without giving a thought to my old infatuation in a wartime summer. That was certainly not why I went, but once there I naturally couldn't resist looking her up in the telephone directory. I hesitated to do it because it seemed ridiculous. Who said she still lived in Paris after so many years? I could remember her new surname, which was not at all new any more. There was only one entry under that name. I found her street on my city map and thought I would call by one day, but kept postponing it.

One Sunday afternoon I took it into my head to go out to the Bois de Boulogne, where I had not been before. I took the metro to Porte Maillot and stood at a loss on a corner staring at the map and at the roundabout and high modern buildings and the motorway that cut through everything with its endless stream of cars. Finally I hailed a taxi and asked the driver to take me to Lac Inférieur. I strolled beside the lake where people were out in rowing boats or lying under the pines by the shore, couples and groups of young people and families with dogs, children and cool-bags.

I regretted going out there. It had turned warm and I had too many clothes on. It had been cloudy when I left the hotel, I had even gone back for a sweater. The heat and my clothing increased the feeling of being in the wrong place. I felt lonesome here where no one was on their own. Until then I had not felt lonely, I was alone, but that is something else.

It struck me how many years I had lived like them. I was at work all the week doing something that did not really interest me, in order to be able to buy a lot of things I didn't really have any use for. On Sundays I went on outings with my family or up to the summer cottage, in a pine wood parcelled out into plots so you could see the other families in the other summer cottages, exactly like the suburban road where we lived then.

I had never said it to anyone, but sometimes it had seemed so futile to work the whole week to be able to spend Sunday messing about, playing ball with my son, seeing to a fence and having lunch under the garden umbrella. Life was to be lived on Sundays and in the holidays, but now and then it felt so strangely weightless. I could feel as far away as if I saw everything on film even though I was fond of my children and both my wives and in general have been fairly satisfied with my life. I was always relieved when Monday came round again so I could go to work. But now I was walking along feeling an outsider by a lake on the edge of the Bois de Boulogne, looking at the families with small children and grandparents and young couples in rowing boats on the lake, where there was a small island with a restaurant and further down a waterfall surrounded by dark, wet rocks covered with moss.

I missed being part of a family like these, with nothing else to do but being together and taking walks and sitting in the sun feeling bored on a Sunday in May like this one. Either you long to go out or you long to be inside. Either you long to be away, nowhere in particular, just away, or you long to be back home. But I was away, far away from it all at long last after many years, and I had nothing at all to go home to apart from a silent apartment where I myself had chosen the furnishings down to the smallest detail, for the first time incidentally, since I had left home at eighteen. I was on the verge of feeling sorry for myself, something I am not prone to usually, and I didn't like it.

At one point I got lost along a road full of parked cars that came to an end behind the grandstand of the race track at Auteuil. A woman was grooming a horse behind the wire fence. Far away on the other side of the stand and beyond some immense stretches of grass I saw a big yellow balloon going up. When I tried to take a short-cut back I ended up again on the edge of the sunken motorway where cars raced along chasing each other's heels. I felt relieved when I found my way to the Porte de Passy and was again walking along an ordinary street with ordinary houses where the emptiness of Sunday seemed less persistent.

I sat down on the terrace outside a bistro. I sipped a glass of beer, cooling off and listening to the voices at surrounding tables, perfectly content not to understand what they said. Earlier I had felt quite sad walking by myself, a foreigner and stranger among the Sunday families on the edge of the Bois de Boulogne, now I felt at ease again in my role as an observer of life as it was lived here. Others' lives, or rather the fragments of others' lives I was observing from my corner table under the awning. A laugh, a smile, a passing gesture that I would remember while those concerned would no doubt have forgotten them. Faces which next moment had gone on, swallowed up by the peaceful afternoon stream in the sunlight that filtered through the plane leaves in a tangled web of green and yellow.

I sat leafing through my little book with its map of every district in Paris to find out exactly where I was. That was how I discovered that she was living in the same district. I went inside and called her number, and to my surprise she answered the phone. I don't really know why that should have surprised me. She herself did not sound very surprised, as I might have expected, cool as ever, I almost said, although in reality I had no means of comparison. I asked if she could remember our meeting that time in the street. I was quite close by, I said. She said she would come and meet me.

This time I had difficulty recognising her, this elderly lady who stopped in front of the café half an hour later and looked around searching for me. She wore very large dark sunglasses and her hair was combed back and bound at the neck in a slightly old-fashioned style. She was one of those older women whose hair turns grey unnoticeably because the blondeness has already faded and wilted a little, rather like straw or rope that has been left out in the sun and rain. I could hear from her speech that she must have lived in France for many years. She expressed herself hesitantly in Danish and used certain words and phrases that became outdated long ago.

I gradually recognised her when she took off her dark shades; her unusually blue eyes, her broad face and her smile. Her voice had changed, it had grown cracked and slightly hoarse, as happens in older women. But what am I saying? After all, she was only a year or two older than I am. The couple of years that make all the difference when you are an overgrown lad who doesn't know how to cope with his passion for a young woman, though strictly speaking she is his own age. I asked what she would have to drink. She wanted a glass of rosé, I ordered another beer, a bit embarrassed over my bad French, which she was tactful enough not to emphasise by ordering herself.

For some years her husband had been posted in Paris working for a large firm, and she had stayed here after they divorced. They had a son who lived in Denmark, where he had married and had his own family. She had originally trained as a nurse, and in later years was sent abroad by an aid organisation. She had travelled all over Asia in that way. I observed her as she spoke and made my replies to her questions as brief and professional as possible. I have never liked talking about myself, and after all we had only spent a few summer weeks together.

The whole of our life was between us, hers and mine, without any points of contact at all. Because we had not kept in touch during the intervening years, I realised all the more strongly now what time does to a face and a body in the form of wear and tear and decay. But in fact we both recovered quite quickly from our amazement. It was like a kind of formality to be overcome. In just a few moments our reunion seemed a matter of course, as if the life we had each lived had been no longer than a summer holiday. It was almost familiar to be sitting like this opposite each other on the terrace of a Parisian café. The world suddenly changes with an abrupt, unexpected shift like a sudden landslide, and yet it is still the same reality with tables and chairs and cars driving past, and waiters in black waistcoats and white aprons.

The unease I felt was not so much due to the fact that I had found my way to her in this gigantic town, where I had nothing special to do and only went where the spirit and my curiosity led me. But there was one thing we both knew we should have to talk about at some point. Something I myself had only thought about now and then, at night when I couldn't sleep or in those rare but sudden occasions during the day when you fall prey to an involuntary recollection. Otherwise I have always chosen to look forward, but I met her again at a point in my life where there is not so terribly much to look forward to. On the other hand I have to admit that my past has never seemed more distant with all its inevitable, inscrutable facts.

I am quite forgetting that of course she was observing me too. I didn't think she meant it when she said I looked just the same. Nobody looks just the same when ten or twenty years have passed, certainly not after a lifetime. No matter how dull and unvarying the personality may be. There was so much we did not know about each other, and which we did not need to know. But was it really so momentous, this thing we slowly circled around and approached as we talked about my uncle the consultant, and his wife, my aunt, long since dead, and the house we had stayed in together for a few summer weeks? An episode of our early youth, should it really be seen as a decisive event?

I had never regarded it as such myself. And

she? I had to ask myself that when I met her clear, cool gaze, surrounded by the ageing face which had only its contours in common with the girl I had briefly known, with broad cheekbones and white, swinging breasts in the semi-darkness behind the open window of the summer cottage bathroom. It was the girl who looked at me through the older woman's face with her blue, searching eyes.

She lived nearby, just round the corner in fact, on the Boulevard de Beauséjour. She invited me home for a cup of tea. As we walked through the impressive entrance hall with its wrought iron and marble and up the stairs to the elevator, I noticed the birthmark in the hollow of her knee, just visible through the fabric of her tights under the dark skirt. It was a sumptuous apartment from the turn of the century, and from the windows in the high-ceilinged room there was a view over the trees in the park to the other side of the street.

It was a large apartment, I could hear, as

her steps resounded on the parquet floor of the corridor. I didn't understand why she liked living alone in such a big apartment. The living room was furnished with antiques and oriental carpets. It looked as if it hadn't been altered for decades. The sky had clouded over again and a subdued green light filled the room. I caught sight of myself in a gold-framed mirror above the stove in the corner. I thought I looked old in that lifeless room, stooping and bald in my casual jacket. A distant rumble sounded. At first I thought it was a plane, but when it came again I could hear it was thunder.

We sat in front of the open door to a narrow balcony that ran the whole length of the façade. The low iron railings were shaped into twining arabesques that blended with the foliage and branches of the trees above. Through them we could see solitary figures passing by down on the gravel paths of the park. Older men and women with children in buggies or hand in hand. Now and then a cool breeze made the thin curtains swell up for a moment before they again collapsed. A flash of lightning was followed by a clap of thunder, this time closer. Then the first heavy drops of rain began to fall, faster and faster until they veiled the view in shining threads of water.

As I said, we told each other very little

about our lives, but how much is there to tell when all is said and done? Long stretches, whole decades, can easily be wrapped up in a couple of sentences. On the other hand, a single sentence can cover a whole story if it seems really worth the telling. She obviously did not feel that about her life, and for my part I was inclined to agree with her. Her husband had left her and moved back to Denmark when he met a younger woman. She had started to work, something she hadn't done since they moved to Paris.

She talked about her times in Asia. Some years before that she had spent a month or two in north-eastern India, close to the Bangladeshi border. The rain fell faster, it had grown almost dark outside and still darker in the room, which was occasionally illuminated by a purplish-blue flash of lightning. I watched a young Japanese couple come running, guide-books over their heads, to seek shelter under one of the trees. When

I looked down again they had gone. There had been villages in the Ganges delta accessible only by the narrow paths in the system of embankments that separated the paddy fields in a labyrinthine pattern of squares. She had noted the flooded fields from the plane when she landed in Calcutta.

It had been riveting, she said, to sit on the back of a motorcycle, a woman in her sixties, and drive between the outspread enclosures of standing water reflecting the sky, divided by the embankments that were paved with brick to prevent them crumbling during the monsoon. Sometimes she caught sight of an ox with twisted horns standing in the water up to its chest, reflected to the last detail from horn to tail tuft. She looked at me and I knew we were both picturing another landscape.

When I think of her I like best to imagine her sitting astride a motorbike, grey-haired and old, with her arms round the waist of a young Indian driving her out into the Ganges delta.

She has put everything she knows behind her, after the man she had come to live with has deserted her. As she sits on the back of the motor-bike rushing along the paths on the embank-ments, nothing is left of the life she has lived for so many years. There is only the memory of that summer when she cycled along a similar path, surrounded by water, on the other side of the world and across the years, on one of the blind alleys of youth.

We sat on, as the sky darkened and the rain slackened and then increased in strength again. A flash of lightning lasted long enough for me to see its branches, crooked and thinner at the ends like the cracks in a wall. As time passed we could barely see each other, we were no more than two voices above the rain and the near or distant thunder. You must have won-dered, she said, why I disappeared so suddenly. She would have liked to say goodbye to me, but I hadn't been there when, without warning, she decided to go home. I did not reply. I studied the silhouette in the chair in front of the open veranda door. Her face almost merged into the shadows around us.

She asked if I could remember the deserted shed I had shown her, right at the end of the flooded meadows at the bottom of the fjord. Perhaps I might remember the English plane that had crashed near there, and what they had said in the village about it? That a parachute had been found not far away. I nodded in the twilight, but she probably did not see that. She described how she had found the English pilot. I let her go on. This was the first time she had told anyone about it, she said, after a pause. She had imagined they might have shot him at some other place.

She had thought of confiding in my uncle. She had decided to do this when she cycled home through the night for the second time. But my uncle and aunt were not up when she woke in the morning, and when she had gone to the bathroom she could feel how tired she was after two sleepless nights. She went to bed again and didn't wake up until past lunchtime. There was no one at home except the housekeeper, who said that some German soldiers had come and asked my uncle and aunt to accompany them.

I let her talk without interrupting her. The rain had stopped, only a distant rumble of thunder still sounded. There was hardly any traffic in the streets this Sunday evening in Passy. It was so quiet I could hear the dripping leaves over in the park, where the lamps had been lit.

She had cycled through the plantation, but at the end of the path a German troop transporter was parked, blocking the way, surrounded by soldiers. She turned round and rode back, trying to remember if she had left anything behind in the shed which might have set the Germans on her trail. She asked herself if anyone could have seen her when she was cycling through the plantation and across the meadows in the night. The house was still empty when she got back. The housekeeper was in the kitchen. She went up to her room, packed her case and wrote a note to my aunt which she left on the dining-room table before creeping out of the house.

She had cycled all the way to the station with her case balanced on the steering wheel, afraid of being caught up with. She took a local train to the nearest big town and had to wait several hours for the connection to Copenhagen. She didn't get home until early next morning. Her mother had scolded her for leaving too soon, and said she would seem ungrateful. Incidentally, my aunt did not employ her mother again.

We sat in silence for a few moments. Then she asked if anyone had suspected her after she went home. I said no. The letter she had left, I said, obviously must have reassured my uncle and aunt.

She had thought about the English pilot

on her way back in the train through the summer night. It was only then that she had really begun to think about him. She recalled his frightened face when he woke up and saw her standing before him in one of the fans of sunlight that penetrated the cracks in the planks of the shed. She thought of his smile and his warm hands, their softness and the strange feel of his stubble on her face the following night. She thought about his being the first man to touch her, the first she had kissed, and she decided that she would never tell anyone about it.

I met her only that once. She asked how long I was staying in Paris and we talked of meeting again. She gave me her telephone number, but I did not call her. Much later she took the trouble of finding my address so she could send me the pilot's cigarette case when she realised she was about to die. I caught sight of the announcement of her death by chance over a year ago. It merely gave her dates: Copenhagen 1927–Paris 1999. The notice was signed *The Family.*

She had not mentioned any family apart from her mother, long since dead, and her ex-husband, who she probably didn't regard as family any more, and their son. We did not talk about our children. As I said, on the whole we did not talk about the intervening years, although they may have meant most to us both. We talked about ourselves at that time, about how young we had been, and we talked about the English pilot. She talked. She told me she had thought about him every day in all the years that had passed. She had felt slightly ashamed of being so wrapped up in that story, just because she herself had happened to be a part of it.

After the war she had seen the same pictures that everyone else saw, from the camps, of skeletal people in heaps, dead, and of other skeletal people with huge prominent eyes, who had barely managed to survive and who looked into the camera with a wondering, questioning expression. They looked as if they were no longer sure whether they were really human beings. As if they dared not believe that someone who saw a picture of them would be able to imagine they had once walked along the streets of an ordinary town with ordinary clothes on their bodies, ordinary bodies in a chance, ordinary life. She had looked at the pictures and felt ashamed, although she had played no part in the sufferings of those people.

She had felt shame because she had taken no part either in their sufferings or their survival. The war, that had happened in another place, and her own story was so infinitesimally unimportant. A young woman's first love story. She felt ashamed of her worries about the English pilot, who most probably had been treated as a prisoner of war and not like one of those living skeletons, who should have been dead and realised that themselves. Presumably he had gone home to his town in England, emaciated maybe, but not nearly so emaciated as those others and not nearly so amazed at being alive, and no doubt he had soon met a nice girl and made her pregnant.

She could have tried to find him, to find out who had hidden there and no doubt was still hiding behind the initials *M.W.* on the cigarette case, but she didn't. She let the years pass and she thought of him when there was nothing else to think about. He was the idea beneath all her fleeting, passing thoughts, and that was what he remained, a thought more than a memory, for in time she couldn't remember what he had looked like. She had never seen him outside the shed, only in its half-light that morning when she found him, and a couple of nights after that when they had come close to each other, two shadows among the shadows.

He had talked to her, but she had not understood half of what he said, and had forgotten the rest. How strange, that she had forgotten what her first lover told her. It was their love she remembered, her own and his, which she had felt like a warmth and a softness in his hands and in his low, half unintelligible voice.

I felt ashamed too, on my way down in the elevator. That was why I did not call her again. The asphalt of the Boulevard de Beauséjour was black and gleaming in the orange street light, like a black mirror that only reflected the darkened outline of things. For over fifty years I'd believed she had gone home early from her holiday at my uncle and aunt's summer cottage because I had betrayed her pilot. I could have told her, but I kept silent. What good would it have done? The fact that I was innocent in her eyes only made my guilt feeling worse. That my guilt was so to speak in vain merely increased it, now that I had failed to tell her my part of our story. To tell her that it was ours and not hers alone.

I went to visit her grave. I will not go into how I discovered it, but I can say this much, it was difficult. People can be hard enough to find when alive, but it is all the harder when they are dead. I had to search for a long time, although I had been given directions at the cemetery office. I was not geared up for visits to churchyards, I have never been able to see the point of them and as far as possible avoid going to funerals unless I am forced into it.

It was a cold, wet day in November, and drops fell from the heavy branches of the trees under the lowering sky. If I had believed that the dead possess some form of consciousness I would have felt sorry for them, lying all on their own alongside the gravel paths, each in their plot, rather like being in a residential district that can be just as grey and deserted on an autumn day such as that. But there she was, beneath a shining slab of Greenland marble. A half-withered bouquet lay on the grave, of roses, dark red, almost brown.

I had brought a bunch myself, Dutch tulips, you can always get those. I placed them beside the withered bouquet and hurried to get away. Suddenly it felt completely wrong and misguided to put flowers on the grave of a woman I had really never known other than in a peripheral and short-lived meaning of the word. Slightly bashful over my sentimental impulse, I regretted going out there at all, and using time and energy searching her out at her last address. It suddenly seemed like an untimely attempt to demonstrate a bond that had never been there.

All the same, I did go back. You would think I had other things to see to, and in fact I have, although I readily admit it can be a hard job to fill in time when you are retired. The diary columns of days and hours stand there shouting out for a content, no matter what, empty and uniform as they are. Although the years pass more quickly when you are older, the days can be long and demanding, with holes that have to be avoided. I can't give a proper explanation of why I went back and there probably isn't one. Perhaps it was curiosity about the half-withered bouquet of roses I had seen on the grave.

I went there again, not once but several times, with a couple of weeks or a month between visits. I always took flowers, and each time there was a bouquet of fresh or withered roses on her gravestone. The oldest bouquets were removed as new ones arrived, my own or the other visitor's. I was convinced there were only two of us. In a spontaneous impulse I had decided on red roses myself the second time, and roses it was from then on. It developed into a positive dialogue of roses in which we took turns to place a fresh bouquet and remove the one that had withered, I and the unknown other.

One afternoon at the end of February it had begun to snow when I arrived. As usual I took away the last half-withered bouquet, not knowing whether it was mine or the other person's, before laying the bouquet I had arranged in place in front of the gravestone and was about to leave. He stood a step or two behind me, I had not heard him.

He smiled, almost shyly, and it struck me that the shyness both suited and did not suit him. It was becoming because it brought out something boyishly emotional in his otherwise inscrutable, masculine face, while at the same time it did not suit his erect and immaculate appearance, the silver-grey hair combed back from the high brow, and the freshly shaven, lined face. He had narrow lips, a pointed chin and what is known as an aristocratic profile. He was sun-tanned and wore a pale blue shirt and a striped tie, I could see, inside the turned-up collar of his dark coat. It had been many years since I'd felt any need to wear a tie.

He looked about my age, maybe even slightly older, but he was the kind of man you would say looked good for his age. His roses hung head-down at the end of one arm, the other was hidden behind his back. He walked past me without saying anything, as if he had been standing in a queue, and took his time over it, squatting down to place his bouquet correctly beside mine on the gravel around the gravestone. He might have been giving me the chance to disappear before he turned round again.

I stayed where I was, I cannot explain why, whether out of curiosity, or because I had come to see him as a rival, post-mortem so to speak, and was being stubborn. He stood up and stayed for a moment with bent head looking down at the burnished stone, where the snow-flakes lodged in the grooves of the bronze letters that formed her name. Then he turned abruptly and stretched out his hand:

'I don't think we know each other . . .'

We walked together along an avenue separating the sections of the churchyard. He was half a head taller than me. He kept screwing up his eyes, and at first I thought the snowflakes bothered him, but he kept on doing it when we reached the inn, built as part of an anonymous housing block opposite the entrance to the churchyard. We sat by a bay window, he ordered whisky for us both. The panes were of thick brown glass, they gave the snowflakes a coppery light, and weakly reflected the daylight.

Not many guests were to be seen in the dim light. From an adjoining room you could hear the little clicks of billiard balls, and in one corner a thin old man sat by himself. He wore a hospital gown under his coat and a plaster on his neck; in the centre of the plaster was a little ventilator. A dog with a long coat lay on the threadbare wall-to-wall carpet beside another man sitting with his back to us at the bar talking to the barmaid. You could see his fat white builder's arse in the gap between his trousers and vest.

I turned back to the man on the other side of the table. It had seemed somehow natural, as we stood beside her grave in the snow and he suddenly asked me to have a drink with him. He had asked who I was and how long I had known his ex-wife.

'Fifty-seven years, that is a long time,' he smiled. Longer than he had known her himself. But she had never talked about me. I said we had known each other when we were young. We walked towards the exit at the end of the avenue. Later on we lost contact, I said. The snowflakes flew around each other in wide circles in front of the dark cypresses of the avenue.

'A youthful love affair?'

He surprised me with his spontaneous manner, but strangely enough there was something that inspired confidence in the way he looked so directly at me. Perhaps it was the involuntary tics at the corners of his eyes that softened the power of his clear, confronting gaze. I smiled back. You could say that. But how had we met? I explained the circumstances and he nodded, almost approvingly.

The barmaid brought us our whisky. We sat in silence for a while. Two elderly, well-preserved men in a suburban pub which neither of us would normally have dreamed of patronising. I wondered whether to tell him about the English airman. He looked into his glass and turned it in his sun-tanned hands. He must have noticed both of us looking at his hands. Spain . . . He had just come back from a winter holiday. They had a house down there, he and his new wife.

'I still call her my new wife,' he said with

a wry smile, looking out at the circling snowflakes. I visualised the grave we had been standing by half an hour earlier.

They had met a few years after the war. They came from very different backgrounds. He looked up at me and his smile was slightly shy again. He had enjoyed a comparatively privileged childhood. I could tell he was a man accustomed to choosing his words with care, his speech was as correct and well-groomed as his outward appearance. He placed his hands flat on the table. His parents were against it, but he had followed his heart. He said it a bit awkwardly, the word 'heart', as if he needed to turn the cliché in his hands once or twice before he could bring himself to drop it into the conversation.

He had done what he could to make her comfortable in the strange surroundings into which he had brought her. At first she had been uncertain how to cope with his friends. Spoilt and carefree contemporaries, who drove their own cars and dressed for dinner. He protected her from the eyes arrogantly sizing her up. He tried to compensate for what he took to be her fear of falling short, which showed itself in an air of reticence at parties. Her silence could seem almost haughty and rude when they were out somewhere and she just sat there without joining in the conversation. He had insisted on visiting her and her mother at home, although for a long time she would not introduce him. The dressmaker had been still more morose and unapproachable. He often had to take charge of the conversation himself, until his throat was dry from talking while the two women sat listening.

For a long time he had interpreted her reserve as an inferiority complex, but later came to understand it as pride, which probably came to the same thing. He could never make it out. He sighed. He had never really made her out. They were married a year after they met. He proposed on a Sunday, they were out for a walk in the park. They sat on a bench, she gazed at the lawns in silence. She asked why he wanted her. Because he loved her, he had replied. Yes, but why?

He had not known how to answer. Instead he kissed her. She looked at him wonderingly, and finally she smiled, a little flat, forced smile, and said yes, but she was still more introverted in the period leading up to the wedding and during their honeymoon. They had been to Rome and stayed at the Hassler. He smiled wryly. He had dragged her around the Roman ruins, the silent young woman he loved, while burning inwardly with the same question she had put to him. Why had she agreed to marry him?

He did not think she had accepted him purely for the sake of the money and access to a better future than her mother's cramped flat in a side street near the harbour could offer. He was sure her pride would have held her back, and she changed almost in the course of one day when they were home and had begun to settle into the apartment he had found in a pleasant district. It almost seemed as if she had determined to be cheerful and affectionate, but he allowed himself to be convinced by her loving presence because he needed it.

They were happy for a time. He thought she had been happy too when their son was born and for a few years afterwards. At first the older women of his family reassured him that it was only natural for the baby to claim all her attention, and she was really a very good mother to the little boy, although she started to grow distant and silent again when they were alone. In company with others she surprised him with her liveliness and her ability to express a personal opinion about things, but with him she was again reserved and dreamy.

So the years passed, more or less. You could not say their relationship was actually bad, but there was always the same imperceptible distance, as if she constantly slid away from him even when he held her in his arms. It was best when they were out travelling. They had been to many places, and when they stood watching a Canadian waterfall or went snorkelling over a reef in Thailand he had felt her curiosity about their surroundings infected him as well. Somehow she caught sight of him again abroad, as if he himself was a foreigner who was permitted for a while to embrace her and hug her and hold her gaze. But when they came home her eyes and thoughts were again somewhere else, he did not know where, perhaps in Canada or Thailand, perhaps somewhere that had no name at all because it was not a real place but only a feeling of distaste and longing.

He worked long hours even during the early years, and felt conscience-stricken at being away from home so much. As the boy gradually grew up, she seemed to lose interest in him as well. She could sit for hours at a time in an armchair by the window, while the maid looked after their son. He had hoped things would change when they moved to Paris, where he had been appointed to run a department of the firm of which he was vice chairman. He had hoped they could find each other again in a strange city. And then Paris . . .

He smiled, a little apologetically, and paused. The old man in the hospital gown sat smoking and gazing ahead of him in a trance. A hissing, whistling sound came from his throat when he inhaled. The dog lying beside the bar raised its head and opened its mouth when the barmaid held out a piece of sausage. Its long fur stuck between its black lips as it gobbled up the morsel. I kept silent, waiting for him to go on. He turned to the barmaid and ordered two more whiskies.

Perhaps it had been the mistake of his life to accept the post in Paris. They never made any mutual friends and chiefly met up with his business acquaintances at cocktail parties and dinners at restaurants. Sometimes their parents and old friends came from Copenhagen to visit them, but she must have been lonely when the boy was at school and he himself was at work, often until late in the evening.

'But she didn't do anything herself . . .'

He finished his drink and tightened his lips.

She just grew more and more silent and preoccupied, and when he tried to approach she withdrew to her room, or yielded so passively and with such a distant expression that he only felt still more alone. They had had separate rooms for several years.

He asked if I was married. I replied that I had been married twice. He smiled approvingly, my reply seemed to inspire confidence. If the intention of a marriage was not that you slept together and felt cosy together, he didn't know what was. He emptied his glass. I couldn't help liking his modesty. 'Feel cosy together', of course he was right.

'With the years . . .' he said and interrupted

himself. 'If as a man, you don't . . .'

He fidgeted with his glass a bit. I knew very well what he was talking about.

'Of course they say, it's different for women . . .'

The ice cubes clinked in the empty glass. He had met a woman. He looked at me and I could almost feel him reading my face. She was fifteen years younger. She worked in the accounts department at his office and had just been divorced.

'Yes, it's as banal as it can be,' he smiled. 'One more whisky?'

I said no thanks. He ordered one for himself.

It wasn't because he had consciously been looking for another woman, he was not like that at all. I shook my head, although I had not the least reason to shake my head or to nod, for that matter.

'But unconsciously . . .'

He shrugged his shoulders.

They were together in his office, in the evenings, or in his car. She had lived with her parents after her divorce. Now and then they met at a hotel near the Gare du Nord, or drove out of Paris and spent the night at an inn, if he could get away with it. At one point he rented a small apartment at the other end of town, near Nation. That was more bearable than the scruffy hotels where they showed no surprise if you only wanted a room for a couple of hours. Yet it had been humiliating for them both, and for his wife, of course, even if she didn't know anything.

His double life lasted a couple of years. Now it was his turn to sit gazing into the distance at the dinner table. They were alone now, their son was back in Denmark at boarding school. He asked if I could imagine what it had been like to sit alone together in a big apartment in Passy talking of nothing or not saying anything at all as he thought about the other woman who had taken him into her arms a few hours earlier in a hotel room near the Gare du Nord, warm and impatient to press her body close to his.

I pictured them, the couple in the somewhat gloomy apartment on the Boulevard de Beauséjour with its antiques and Persian carpets, and thought that he couldn't know how exactly I was able to imagine the marital scene. I saw similar scenes swiftly cross my inner eye, of other rooms during the course of my life. A similar silence and a similar feeling that the room was closing around you, feeling at the same time that the doors only open outwards, and there would be no way back.

After two years had passed, he told her. His mistress could wait for him no longer. He lied about how long it had been going on. He saw no reason to tell her that. He had believed it would be a relief to show his hand. He had imagined that her anger would make it easier, proud as she was, but she did not get angry, nor did she weep, and he felt no less guilt on that account. Later on they had seen each other only when their son matriculated, and then when he married. She had not wanted to see him, and for many years his son had not wanted to meet his new wife. In fact there had been a long period when he'd had no contact with his son.

Maybe he would have seen it differently if he hadn't been sent to boarding school, although ironically enough it was his mother who had had the idea of sending him away. But in the boy's eyes he was the criminal, he could feel that, even if nothing was ever said. They saw each other only rarely, usually in town, for lunch once in a while. He always had to be the one who suggested they met.

He emptied his glass.

'I don't feel I know him. I would really like to . . . but perhaps that's how it usually is.'

He looked at me.

'Is it?'

I had no chance to reply before he turned

abruptly to the bar and asked the barmaid for the bill. Anyway I did not know what I should answer. He smiled. I must be tired of listening to him. It was snowing fast when we stood in front of the inn and held out our hands.

So it happened that one Sunday I parked my car on a residential road in one of the suburbs north of Copenhagen. The sun shone the way it sometimes does in March, sharp and white so the trees seem still more bare in the clear cold air. When I woke up in the morning I was on the point of ringing to cancel. I told myself I had already gone too far on a wild goose chase that had nothing to do with me. I had no right to allow a complete stranger to bare his soul to me on such flimsy grounds just because he seemed to trust me, and because he obviously needed to tell his story to a detached listener.

I could also have justified my hesitation because really I had no interest in listening to him and in that way learning the details of her life. I had known nothing about it, and in any case it had been played out far away from mine, with no other contact than our brief meeting long ago, before life had properly begun for either of us. But that was not how I thought about it at all and perhaps in reality it was my own curiosity that made me hesitate, because I half reproached myself for it. But curiosity is not the right word. How shall I explain it? Again and again I pictured the submerged meadowland by the fjord and the shed made of sun-blanched, weather-beaten planks, where the English pilot had hidden. In my memory that shed was like a locked casket.

Perhaps it had been the same for her. She had thought about her pilot all through her life, she told me, when together we watched the rain and the lightning over Passy. It had been the first time a man touched her. It had also been the first time I touched a woman when, timidly and fruitlessly, I made my approaches in the semi-darkness between the planks filtering the sunlight in rays and fans. But there have been other women since then, not many but not actually so few, and some have been far more decisive meetings than the first object of my early, fumbling desire. Likewise there could have been so many other, later reasons for her gradual withdrawal from her marriage, mutely and absently, until her husband wavered in the emptiness and silence and reached out one day for the next woman to cross his path.

I could not know anything about that, and so much has happened in my own life that I have not written about here and which has no relevance to that summer during the war. But perhaps you are not searching for reasons at all when you try to look back through the morass of complications and fluctuations, the tangled threads of life, of meetings and shared life and partings, togetherness and break-up, buried dreams, broken or forgotten promises and unexpected openings. Everything you have lived through, sometimes in despair, now and then rejoicing, but for most of the time neither of these.

Perhaps it is something different from explanations that you look for, for how can you ever manage to get your inborn strengths and weaknesses and all the rest of the chaos of circumstances and coincidences to merge into that famous higher unity? Perhaps it is much simpler and at the same time more impenetrable, the experience you are trying to come close to again. I say 'again' because there is in fact a possibility of turning back. To what? To a foundation, I believe, underneath the years and the shining transparencies of memory, all of its confused splinters and flakes of lived life.

I would like to be able to turn back to the background of it all which perhaps does not explain anything but which in itself neither can nor should be explained. For me it has turned into the flooded meadows with tufts of grass in the gleaming water beneath a vast changing sky, a quaking marsh to walk on; but what good is that? After all, I could never actually go back. All I can do is contemplate those early, inaccessible places of memory and know in myself that it was there I stood before everything began to take shape. Before I myself started to form and be formed, with hands and arms buried in the available opportunities, as I was kneaded into it all and changed beyond recognition to those who stayed behind and watched me vanish over the horizon.

I don't know if I thought about all that when I had found the right house number and walked up the paved path in the front garden to ring the door bell. The door was opened by a small woman with dark eyes and grey streaks in her black hair. She smiled shyly and asked me to come in. Even after so many years she didn't seem like someone at ease with herself when she took my coat from me and called to her husband in a slightly flustered way.

I looked around the hall and through the doors to the adjoining rooms. It was a modern house, everything in it was modern, and it was so tidy you couldn't believe anyone lived there. The only sign of life was a sports bag on a chair in the hall with two tennis rackets in it.

'We only moved here a year ago,' she said, smiling shyly.

But although it must be twenty years since she had arrived in this country, she still had a strong accent. While we were flourishing, I thought, she might sometimes have looked around her and wondered how she'd ended up here. How her life had come to be like this. Presumably she was satisfied, anyway I hoped so, but she must have wondered. She too had come far from her deepest foundations, her beginnings, to end up with a man who had already been married and brought a child into the world. She had never had children.

He came downstairs and stretched out his hand to me with a smile, putting a protective arm around her slight shoulders. We went into the living room. She seemed fragile standing beside him in the big room with its rather showy furnishings. He was casually dressed and yet there was something impeccable about his chinos, dark blue pullover and checked shirt. Even his comfortable shoes spoke of leisure wear in an irreproachable manner.

We sat in a garden room with floor to ceiling windows facing the lawn, with its rose-beds and a few fruit trees. We drank white wine, each in our deck chair. We chatted of sporadic things, about Paris then and now and whatever else that came to mind, slightly forced; but he was good at keeping the conversation going.

She said little, but at one point he made her laugh and I could suddenly visualise what she must have looked like when she was twenty years younger, approaching forty and divorced, but still young. Still easily moved to laughter, a young woman with a kittenish smile, attractive and interesting to many men.

She rose to go into the kitchen and serve the meal. He watched her go and then turned to me and held my gaze.

'I love her,' he said, without preliminaries, blinking once or twice. Then he leaned back and gazed at the water-lilies on the pond and the bare branches of the fruit trees.

'But perhaps I should not have allowed myself that,' he went on.

I put down my glass on the table between us.

'Why?'

'Oh,' he said. 'I can't help thinking that. My son . . . they can be tough at times.'

I nodded. He looked at me again.

'But now you will be able to get an impression, he may drop in later, with the children.'

'I didn't think . . .'

He blinked again.

'My son wants to meet you. He would like to meet someone who knew his mother.'

He replenished our glasses and we drank. I

felt a captive in his glass cage with the sun shining fiercely in on us. I regretted that I had come. I had certainly intruded much too far into a world that had nothing to do with me. He regarded me with an almost apologetic expression. He must have read my thoughts. But what was I thinking? That I felt shanghaied into taking part in his family complications? He cleared his throat.

'Perhaps I should have . . .'

I raised my hand in a reassuring gesture.

'It's not that I reproach myself for getting divorced,' he said quietly. 'What I can still reproach myself with is marrying her in the first place. That I just had to have her, that I let her . . . yes, it sounds strange, but that I let her give way. But now let me show you the garden . . .'

We went out onto a terrace also reached from the adjoining dining room. The sun was warm enough for us to be comfortable outside without coats. We went down to the pond, it was half covered over with water-lilies. He pointed to some small bricks heaped beside the pond in a tidy pyramid.

'We had the pond dug out in the autumn. It was quite an operation.' He pointed. 'I have thought of making a path all the way round. And in the spring I'll get some goldfish.'

I picked up one of the bricks. It was well squared, with perfectly even sides.

'It is sett paving,' he said. 'Hardly anyone makes it any more. I dare not tell you how much this heap has cost me. But it is to be my silver wedding gift. Dénise has always wanted a pond with goldfish in it.'

We walked around the pond. He blinked, looking down, and I had to screw up my own eyes against the strong sunlight. He sighed.

'Life is strange, isn't it? I dragged a Danish woman to Paris with me, only to desert her there. True, it was by her own choice, she did not want to come home. And later I dragged a Frenchwoman to Denmark, where she is still considered a wicked witch.'

I felt sorry for him, held in the grip of his conscience. I thought of the roses he took to his ex-wife's grave at least twice a month. I was the only one who knew he had brought those roses, which no one except the gardeners and grave-diggers and chance passers-by ever saw.

I told him about her meeting with the English pilot and about my shameful role in the story. I did it as much for my own sake as his, to make a kind of balance between us. I said she had thought of him every day since that time. When I finished speaking we stood for a while in silence, until Dénise came out on the terrace to tell us lunch was ready. I could see that my tale had made an impression on him and asked myself whether I might have led him onto the wrong track. The only person who could have given an answer lay under a polished slab of Greenland marble.

And perhaps even she would have been at a loss for an answer.

That she had really thought about her English pilot every day was in itself probably an exaggeration. There must have been weeks and whole months when she had not given him a thought. But perhaps he had been an image in her faulty recollection of something deep within herself. Something that had remained unknown, hidden in darkness, and which she needed to bind to a place, a point in time and a face, however unclear to her, in the semi-darkness between the planks of the shed out in the flooded meadows at the end of a fjord by the North Sea, one summer during the war.

The conversation went surprisingly smoothly at the table, considering that we hardly knew each other at all. My host recounted anecdotes his wife must have heard a hundred times before, but she listened almost adoringly, and I thought: there is a happy man. Towards me she was bashful and reticent. He was the one who talked most, he was obviously used to being the centre of things. He seemed relaxed, as if he had been relieved of a burden. It lasted until the door bell rang. She looked at him, he lowered his eyes and hesitated a moment, then rose.

'My son,' he said, stroking her shoulder as he passed to go and open the door.

Shrill voices could be heard in the hall and

the next moment two children rushed into the room. They played tag around the table, a boy of about seven and a girl slightly younger. They were both fair-haired and pasty, and the boy was a bit overweight. The girl tugged excitedly at the handle of the sliding glass door and ran into the garden, followed by her big brother. The outside air was cold and the wind caught the dining-room curtains and made them flutter. Dénise had risen to look at the children, who chased each other through a rose bed, breaking several of the bare branches.

'Zut alors, les roses! . . . Mais non!' she exclaimed indignantly.

A wail came from the garden, the girl must have pricked herself on a rose bush. Her father was already on his way out, a heavily built, stocky man in jogging gear. He looked to be in his mid-thirties but was already half bald. He rushed round the room without regard for us and ran out to the bawling child.

My host followed him. The boy stood beside the pond watching the scene. The father picked up the girl and carried her back to the house followed by the grandfather, who was saying something I could not hear, throwing out his arms in a clumsy, apologetic gesture. His son carried the screaming girl into the next room and laid her on a sofa. She had lost one of her shoes, her grandfather picked it up off the grass. He closed the sliding door after him when he came in.

'Is there a pair of tweezers in the house?' the son shouted, turning towards us angrily.

Dénise hurried into the hall. My host stood in the doorway between the two rooms. She came back with the tweezers. The girl sobbed as her father bent over her ankle.

'I can't see it,' he growled.

His father made a vague gesture with the little shoe.

'Perhaps she has just pricked herself . . .'

'Of course there's a thorn,' the son mumbled

savagely. 'Why the hell would she be crying otherwise?'

The child sniffed but she had stopped crying. My hosts stood in the doorway watching the examination from a distance. A splash sounded from the garden, and then another. The boy stood by the pond throwing bricks into the water. Dénise took a step towards the sliding door. Her husband laid a hand on her arm and went out himself.

From my place at the table I watched him walk calmly across the lawn and bend over the boy, with his hands on his slightly bent knees, it was clear that he was trying to persuade him to stop. The boy took no notice, he went on throwing bricks into the water until he suddenly ran across the lawn and vanished from view.

The grandfather stood for a moment gazing at the water and the water-lilies before turning and going back to the house. His son had given up searching for the thorn in his daughter's ankle, if there had ever been one. He came into the room followed by the child, she was covered in snot and red-eyed. My host joined us.

'Are you hungry?' he smiled.

'We have eaten,' said his son.

'But you could probably use a glass of wine?'

'Rather have a beer.'

His son pulled out a chair and sat down at the table and the little girl crept up onto his lap. Dénise went into the kitchen. I was introduced. The son looked at me without expression. She came back with a beer and two cokes and three glasses on a tray. My host sat down and poured out some wine for her and me before refilling his own glass.

'Let's drink a toast, then,' he said.

I was surprised at how shy he had become. Nor could I understand that it was his son sitting there sizing me up with his small eyes. They bore absolutely no resemblance to each other.

'So you knew my mother?'

'We knew each other when we were young,' I replied.

'She never talked about you.'

He put the bottle to his mouth and drank.

'You didn't see much of each other, you and your mother . . . I mean, in her last years,' his father said.

'What rubbish is that?' replied his son without looking at him. He dried his mouth on the sleeve of his jogging shirt and put the bottle down on the table.

The boy came to the sliding door. He had a tennis racket in each hand. He must have taken them from the bag I had seen on a chair in the hall. He hammered on the pane with the handle of one racket. His grandfather hastened to slide the door open.

'I want to play!' said the boy.

'Not now,' said his father.

'The two of us can play,' said my host cheerfully.

'Come on then!'

They went out onto the lawn. Dénise cleared the table and carried the plates into the kitchen. The girl slid off her father's lap and went over to the sliding door and opened it roughly. I rose and closed it after her. Her father sat in silence picking at the label on his bottle while Dénise took away bowls and dishes. She went in and out once or twice until the table was cleared apart from the wine bottle and glasses.

'I'll go and make some coffee,' she said, leaving the room.

I looked out at her husband standing on the lawn serving one soft easy ball after another, which the boy tried in vain to return with the racket that was far too big for him. The girl sat watching in a garden chair.

'How long have you known my father?'

It was like being subjected to an interrogation. I looked into his flabby face. I didn't like him and I didn't like his kids either. Not many people would agree with me but in my opinion children can be quite as repugnant as adults. On the other hand I realised that I really liked their grandfather, this courteous, authoritative man of the world who winced at his son's hostile glances.

'Not very long,' I replied. 'We didn't meet until after your mother's death.'

He finished his beer and looked out at his father, tirelessly sending tennis balls to the boy in low arcs.

'But you have probably heard how he chucked my mother for her?'

He nodded in the direction of the hall.

'Was it many years ago?'

'What does that matter?'

I couldn't get away from his eyes. He was ugly, I thought, at once correcting myself. Actually he was very ordinary, without any distinctive features. Erased, I thought, as if with an india rubber.

'She never got over it,' he went on,

watching his children and their grandfather.

'She had her work. She travelled . . .'

'But she was lonely.'

'Perhaps she chose to be?'

He leaned towards me, supporting a hand on his knee.

'What do you know about it? She couldn't just go out and find someone new. At her age, I mean, even then . . . it's not so straightforward.'

'Maybe she just didn't want to meet someone else.'

'That's what I'm saying. She was crushed. She loved the bugger, didn't she? And she went on hoping he would come back.'

'Did she?'

'No mistake about that. The way she went on living down there and left everything in the apartment as it was when he scarpered. Shit, it was like going into a museum.'

'You might be wrong, all the same.'

'What d'you mean by that?'

'Perhaps it was not like you think,' I went on.

He looked at me suspiciously.

'There's something I'd like to tell you. But I must ask you to keep it to yourself.'

The story came alive as I told it. There was a place for it in what I knew about her, it fitted. As I listened to myself telling it, I felt it sounded like something that could well be true. And who knows? Perhaps it might really have happened. She must have thought of it as a possibility, at least. I don't know, and I shall never know. Perhaps she did think of the English pilot every day for the rest of her life, as she said. Or was that just something she said because she had met me again so unexpectedly? I was the only one who had any link with the story that perhaps was nothing more than a remote, blurred memory of her youth. The only memory we could have shared.

I told him about my meeting with her in Paris a few years before she died. I told him she had confided in me, maybe because at the same time I was an old friend and yet a stranger, after so many years.

'What I want to tell you about happened long before your parents divorced,' I said. 'You were at boarding school and your father was hardly ever at home. But it was not only that. She told me about their marriage. She had never really been in love with your father, and now, in a strange city . . . The whole thing seemed meaningless to her and had done so for a long time, when she embarked on a relationship with another man. He too was married and had a family. They had met each other before, one summer when they were quite young, but their meeting had been brief. Neither of them expected they would ever see each other again.'

He looked at me with a foolish expression. I could picture it so easily, and I thought he could too. Something you have only heard sounds just as real whether it happened or not, and a lie is sometimes indistinguishable from what could have been true, even to the one who hears himself lying. I paused and let him sit for a while taking in his mother's infidelity, before I continued.

'In the end it was clear that her lover did not intend to desert his family, and he broke off the affair. I don't know if your father ever discovered anything. There were a few years during which he tried to reach her and breathe life into their relationship, but she rejected him. It was only a marriage outwardly when he met Dénise.'

I stopped talking. There were tears in his eyes, it had been almost too much. He looked like a child as he sat opposite me, hunched over his jogging suit. The others came back and we had coffee in the garden room. Dénise had baked a tart.

They left shortly afterwards, my host saw them off. From where I sat I could see them over the hedge between the garden and the road. The young, half bald man hesitated a moment, then he embraced his father, awkward and clumsy, before quickly getting into his car. Dénise saw that as well. I would like to have visited them again, I think we could have become close friends, but I never called back the few times he left a message on my answering machine, and in the end he stopped ringing.

When I arrived home that evening I took out the English pilot's cigarette case. I opened it and picked up the cigarette, the last one he had left, which had remained in the case through all those years. The loose reddish brown shreds of Virginia drifted down onto my knee. I had actually stopped smoking, but I lit the cigarette and took a pull. Naturally it did not taste nice, dried up as it was. I held it between my fingers and watched the smoke twist up through the air like a transparent ribbon winding itself into spirals and bows in the afterglow of the evening sun.

JENS CHRISTIAN GRØNDAHL is one of the most celebrated and widely read writers in Europe. Born in Denmark in 1959, his literary work includes thirteen novels, essays and several plays. Two of his novels, *Lucca* and *Silence in October* were published recently by Canongate. His fiction has been translated into sixteen languages.

ANNE BORN is a translator, poet and poetry publisher. Among her translations are Karen Blixen's *Letters from Africa*, Henrik Stangerup's *Brother Jacob*, short-listed for the European Translation Prize, Per Petterson's *To Siberia*, Jens Christian Grøndahl's *Silence in October*, *Lucca* and *Virginia*, and work by numerous Scandinavian poets.